Happy Birthday Jamela!

Story & Pictures
by
Niki Daly

CINDY

FRANCES LINCOLN CHILDREN'S BOOKS

Jamela felt like jumping out of her shoes.
Soon it would be her birthday!

"You know, Jamela – I am so happy that you were born,"
said Mama. "Let's have a party to celebrate!"

"You were a lovely fat baby," said Gogo, squeezing Jamela.
"And look at you now – such a big girl!"

The next day they went shopping for birthday clothes.

First, they looked at dresses. Jamela tried on lots … until they found one that was just right for a party girl.

Jamela twirled around like a model. Mama said, "That dress is beautiful – but you can't wear those shoes with it."

Jamela looked at her shoes.

They were her favourites, but they were a bit beaten up.

So they went to a shoe shop packed with shoes
in every colour and style.

    "How about these?" said the sales lady.
"They are our Princess Shoes."

    Jamela looked at the sparkly buckles
and little satin bows. Mama looked
at the price.

    "They're very pretty," said Gogo.

    "Yes, but we need shoes that
Jamela can also wear to school,"
said Mama, giving the shoes
back to the sales lady.

Jamela's heart sank. She LOVED those sparkly
Princess Shoes! The sales lady came back
with a pair of black school shoes.
"Those look nice and strong.
How do they feel,
Jamela?" asked Mama.
"Fine," said Jamela.
But she wanted
to cry.

Alone in her room, Jamela wished that, somehow, when she opened the shoe-box, she'd find the Princess Shoes inside. But when she looked, a pair of strong black school shoes lay there like heavy bricks. They smelt nice – but they could never, ever be birthday girl shoes. Birthday girl shoes had to be pretty. They needed to sparkle and glitter.

Suddenly Jamela had an idea …

She got out her box of treasures.
For ages she'd been collecting
precious beads, sparkly
and glittery bits.
Carefully, she glued beads
all over the shoes
until they
sparkled,
glittered
and shone.

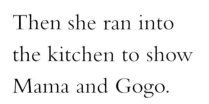

Then she ran into
the kitchen to show
Mama and Gogo.

"Look, Mama!" cried Jamela.

When Mama looked, her eyes almost fell out. "Oh no!" she cried. "What have you done to your new school shoes!"

Gogo wanted to laugh – but wasting money was no laughing matter, so she frowned instead.

"I can't even look at what you've done," said Mama. "*Humba!* Go away, Jamela!" And she waved her arms as though she wanted to sweep Jamela out of the house.

Jamela's lip trembled. She looked around for help, but Gogo pointed to the door. Mama needed time to cool down.

Jamela went outside and sat on the pavement.
She was very, very sad.

When Amin the fruitseller passed by, he asked,
"What's with the long face, Jamela?" So she told him.

"Well, I must say, I like your fancy shoes,
but your mama works very hard and you shouldn't
waste her money."

Just then, someone said, "Wow! Your shoes are absolutely fabulous!"
Jamela looked up. It was Lily the artist from down the road.
"You know what? Those sparkly shoes would sell like
hot cakes on my stall in the market. How would you
like to help me make sparkly shoes?"

Jamela nodded, and managed a little smile.

Early next morning, Jamela and Lily began to decorate some plain shoes that Lily had bought from the supermarket. Lily had bottles and boxes of treasure. Jamela had never seen such wonderful beads.

"What shall we call our shoes?" asked Lily.

"Princess Shoes," said Jamela. She was still thinking about those beautiful shoes she wanted so much.

"Not bad," said Lily. Then she snapped her fingers and announced, "T-raa! I think we should call them 'Jamela Shoes'… after their talented designer!"
Jamela beamed.

That weekend, Lily and Jamela set up their stall in the market. As soon as they unpacked the Jamela Shoes, people started to gather round. No one had ever seen anything quite like them.

The shoes sold like hot cakes. Some girls were still queuing when, finally, the shoes had all gone. But Lily said she'd take orders for more.

At the end of the day, Lily counted up the money, then handed a bundle of notes to Jamela and said, "This is your share… partner!"

Jamela couldn't believe her eyes. She was rich!
Now she could give Mama the money to buy her school shoes.

Mama was amazed to hear that Jamela had been earning money from her sparkly shoes. She gave Jamela a big hug, looked at the notes and said, "This is more than enough for your school shoes."

"You really are full of tricks, Jamela!" cackled Gogo.

On her birthday, Jamela looked beautiful. All her favourite people were there.

When all the presents had been opened, Mama handed Jamela a big, big carrier bag. Jamela dipped in and pulled out a pretty box with a card that read "Happy Birthday, Jamela – from Mama."

Jamela opened it and pretended to be surprised.

"New school shoes!" she cried. "*Enkosi*, Mama!"

"Keep going!" said Mama. "There's something else."
Once more, Jamela dipped into the bag. Another box
and another card!
Jamela read "Happy Birthday, Jamela – from Jamela."
"Open it! Open it, Jamela!" cried Gogo.

Jamela opened the lid – and squealed: "Princess Shoes!"

"Put them on! Put them on!" cried Gogo.

Lily helped Jamela fasten the sparkly buckles.

Jamela stroked the satin bows.

"They really are shoes for a princess," said Mama.
"But I'm very happy that you also have shoes for school."

"And Jamela Shoes for dancing!" said Lily.

"Now who's got lucky feet!" said Gogo.

Everyone sang

Min'emnandi kuwe, Min'emnandi kuwe,
Min'emnandi, Jamela, Min'emnandi kuwe.

Then Jamela blew out seven candles – and made a wish.

GLOSSARY OF XHOSA WORDS

enkosi (en-kor-see) – thank you

humba (hum-bah) – go away

Min'emnandi kuwe (mee-n'em-naarn-dee coo-where) – A happy day to you (sung to the tune of *Happy Birthday to You*)